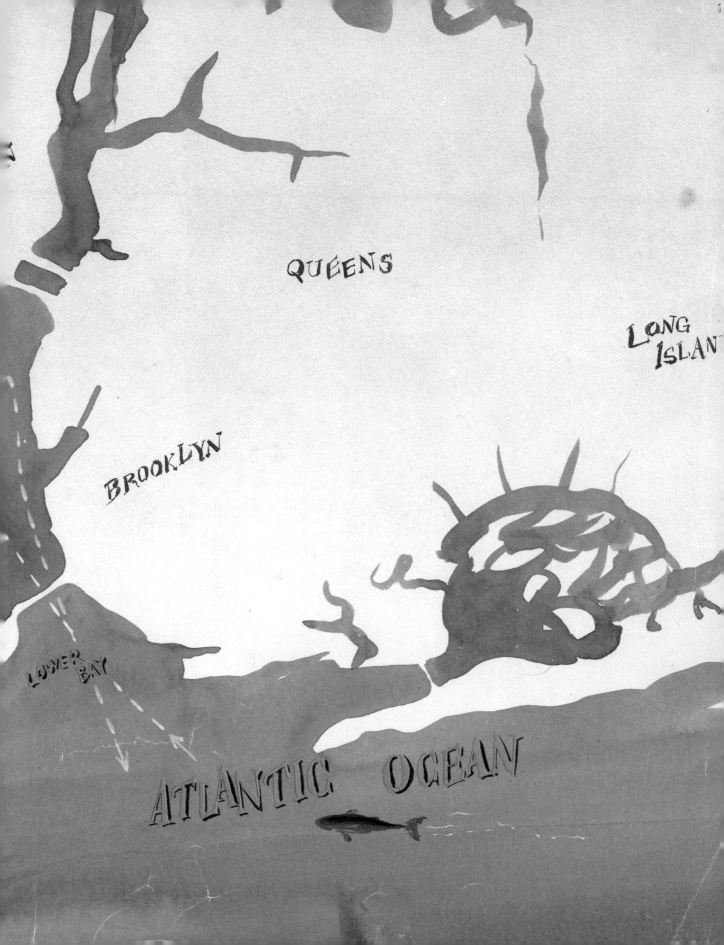

Library of Congress Cataloging-in-Publication Data
Ziefert, Harriet.
 Henry's Wrong Turn / Harriet Ziefert; illustrated by Andrea Baruffi.
  p. cm.
 Summary: In this story based on a true incident, a humpback whale tries to
find its way home after mistakenly swimming into New York Harbor.
 ISBN 0-316-98778-6
 [1. Humpback whale—Fiction. 2. Whales—Fiction] I. Baruffi, Andrea, ill.
 II. Title.
PZ7.Z487Hen 1989
[E]—dc19

Published simultaneously in Canada by Little, Brown & Company (Canada) Limited
Printed in Singapore for Harriet Ziefert, Inc.

HENRY'S WRONG TURN

HARRIET ZIEFERT

ILLUSTRATED BY

ANDREA BARUFFI

LITTLE, BROWN AND COMPANY
BOSTON   TORONTO   LONDON

He was a big humpback whale who made a wrong turn. He was swimming in the ocean, and instead of going out to sea, he turned and went up the Hudson River— right into New York harbor

No one knew why Henry—for that is what someone named him—wanted to be in New York harbor. Certainly there was nothing for him to eat in those waters. But there he was.

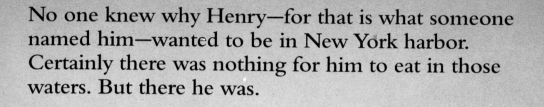

Henry swam under the Verrazano-Narrows Bridge. The day was bright and sunny, and on the bridge, traffic moved right along. No one up there noticed Henry, but down in the harbor, a tugboat captain did. He signaled to all the other boats: *Watch out for the whale!*

There was lots of excitement. No one could remember seeing a whale in New York harbor. Everyone was on the lookout for Henry. But where was he?

"Look! There he is!" shouted one of the visitors to the Statue of Liberty. "Take a good look, everyone, because you probably won't see another one like him again."

The *Queen Elizabeth II* passed Henry on her way to sea.
He was quite small next to the mighty liner. The ship
sounded its horn and Henry again dove under the water.

The Coast Guard wanted to help Henry, so they sent a boat to follow him.

Henry quickly swam away from the patrol boat. He passed an aircraft carrier, *Intrepid*. Visitors on deck cheered when Henry sent up a magnificent spray.

Suddenly, Henry disappeared.

No one saw Henry until evening. By then he was
near the World Trade Center. He seemed lost.
"We've got to help Henry go back to the ocean," the
Coast Guard sailors told each other. "There are
too many boats in the harbor. He could get hit!"

In the twilight, Henry headed past the Battery into
Buttermilk Channel between Governors Island and
Red Hook in Brooklyn.

Two ferries carrying commuters were just leaving their slips. The ferries immediately put their engines in reverse, veered off their courses and...

avoided a collision with Henry!
Now the Coast Guard was back on Henry's tail.
The captain of the cutter was determined to
make him turn around and return to the ocean.

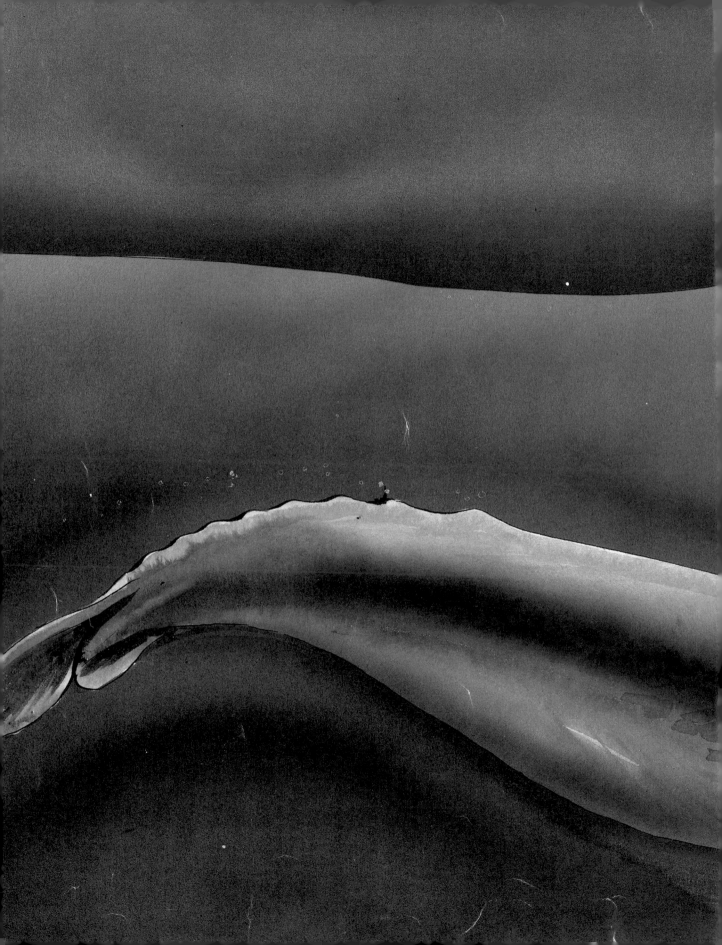

And it worked! Perhaps Henry didn't like the noise from the boat's engines. Perhaps he was hungry. For whatever reason, Henry turned around.

Henry swam fast. By the time the moon was in the sky, he was back at the Verrazano Narrows Bridge, heading out to sea.

Henry left the harbor, then he dove.
"Good luck, Henry!"

HE BLOWS TOWN
AFTER WHALE OF A TIME

After a whirlwind tour of the trendy West Side, Henry the Humpback Whale appeared to be back on course yesterday, headed perhaps for summer in the Hamptons.

Henry, said to be only the second misdirected whale ever to venture into a major urban harbor, traveled up the Hudson River Thursday before turning back near 86th St.

Henry spent a relatively comfortable night off the Jersey coast, trailed by a 41-foot Coast Guard cutter, and Coast Guard petty officer Bob Mascaro said the 35 to 40-foot mammal was expected to continue down the coast "toward Long Island tonight." Which he did.

"He's out to sea and headed east along Long Island," said Sam Sadove, research director of the Okeanos Ocean Research Center in Hampton Bays, L.I., which christened the whale Henry in tribute to Henry Hudson.

—Mark Kreigel, N.Y. Daily News, June 18, 1988